At the
End of the
Garden

Crabtree Publishing Company
www.crabtreebooks.com
1-800-387-7650

PMB 16A, 350 Fifth Ave.
Suite 3308,
New York, NY

616 Welland Ave.
St. Catharines, ON
L2M 5V6

Published by Crabtree Publishing in 2008

Series Editor: Jackie Hamley
Editor: Melanie Palmer
Series Advisor: Dr. Hilary Minns
Series Designer: Peter Scoulding
Proofreader: Reagan Miller

Text © Penny Dolan 2007
Illustration © Martin Impey 2007

First published in 2007
by Franklin Watts
(A division of Hachette
Children's Books)

Printed in Canada/012013/DM20121114

**Library and Archives Canada
Cataloguing in Publication**

Dolan, Penny
    At the end of the garden / Penny Dolan ;
Martin Impey, illustrator.

(Tadpoles)
ISBN 978-0-7787-3850-3 (bound).
--ISBN 978-0-7787-3881-7 (pbk.)

    1. Readers (Primary). 2. Readers--Gardens.
I. Impey, Martin II. Title. III. Series: Tadpoles
(St. Catharines, Ont.)

PE1117.T33 2008   428.6   C2007-907421-9

**Library of Congress
Cataloging-in-Publication Data**

Dolan, Penny.
  At the end of the garden / by Penny Dolan ;
illustrated by Martin Impey.
      p. cm. -- (Tadpoles)
  Summary: A child observes a scarecrow in the
garden in all kinds of weather.
    ISBN-13: 978-0-7787-3850-3 (reinforced lib. bdg.)
    ISBN-10: 0-7787-3850-7 (reinforced lib. bdg.)
    ISBN-13: 978-0-7787-3881-7 (pbk.)
    ISBN-10: 0-7787-3881-7 (pbk.)
    [1. Scarecrows--Fiction.] I. Impey, Martin, ill.
II. Title.
    PZ7.D6978At 2008
    [E]--dc22
                                                        2007049085

At the
End of the
Garden

by Penny Dolan

Illustrated by Martin Impey

Crabtree Publishing Company

www.crabtreebooks.com

Penny Dolan

"I love the way this friendly scarecrow is so happy, having fun with his friends even on the rainiest of days."

Martin Impey

"I love to paint from my studio at the end of the garden, where Mr. Scarecrow Pumpkin-head plays!"

At the end of the garden, what can you see?

A very funny man by
the old apple tree.

He smiles at the wind.

He smiles at the rain.

He smiles when the sun comes out again.

11

In his faded old hat,
there is a robin's nest.

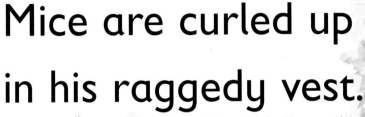

Mice are curled up
in his raggedy vest.

14

He has beetles
in his boots ...

... and frogs for friends.

And he lives way down
where the garden ends.